I Love You Like
Crazy Cakes

WRITTEN BY ROSE LEWIS   ILLUSTRATED BY JANE DYER

I Love You Like
Crazy Cakes

LITTLE, BROWN AND COMPANY
BOSTON   NEW YORK   LONDON

For more information or to begin your own journey, visit www.fwcc.org.

Text copyright © 2000 by Rose A. Lewis
Illustrations copyright © 2000 by Jane Dyer

First Edition

Library of Congress Cataloging-in-Publication Data
Lewis, Rose A.
I love you like crazy cakes / by Rose A. Lewis ; illustrated by Jane Dyer. — 1st ed.
p.   cm.
Summary: A woman describes how she went to China to adopt a special baby girl. Based on the author's own experiences.
ISBN 0-316-52538-3
[1. Intercountry adoption—Fiction. 2. Adoption—Fiction. 3. Babies—Fiction.] I. Dyer, Jane, ill. II. Title.
PZ7.L58787Iaal 2000
[E]—dc21   99-34175

10 9 8 7 6 5 4 3 2 1

TWP

Printed in Singapore

The illustrations for this book were done in watercolor on Waterford 140 lb. hot press paper. The text was set in Eva Antiqua Light and the display type was set in Shelley Andante Script and Eva Antiqua Heavy. Chinese calligraphy on page 32 was done by Victor Ting-Feng Hsu.

For my daughter, Alexandra Mae-Ming Lewis

R. A. L.

For my dear friend, Jan, and her daughter,

Jessica Hee Sook Martyn

J. D.

ONCE UPON A TIME in China there was a baby girl
who lived in a big room with lots of other babies.

The girls shared cribs with one another and became
great friends. The girls had nannies to take care of them,
but each was missing something — a mother.

Far away across the ocean was a woman who also had many friends, but she was missing something, too — a baby. That woman was me.

So I wrote a letter to officials in China and asked if I could adopt one of the babies who lived in the big room.

Months later, I received a letter with a picture of a beautiful baby girl . . . that was you. The people in China said I could adopt you if I promised to take good care of you. I promised I would.

A few weeks later, I packed my suitcases with toys, books, diapers, food, and clothes just for you and boarded a plane for the very long trip to China.

There were other families who were also waiting to meet their babies. I was so excited and nervous. I couldn't wait to hold you.

The next day, your nannies brought you and your friends from the countryside to the city to meet us.

I was so happy that I cried the moment I took you in my arms . . . you cried, too.

I had been waiting for you my whole life.

I brought you back to the hotel and sat you down on the bed to get a good look at you.

You sat up so straight.

Your rosy cheeks made you look like a soft, pink doll.

When you looked at me with those big brown eyes, I knew we belonged together.

"I love you like crazy cakes," I whispered.

How did this happen? How did someone make this perfect match a world away? Did the Chinese people have a special window to my soul?

The first night, I laid you down in your crib made up with crisp white linens and new blankets from America.

I tucked you in and kissed your little hands and tiny feet a hundred times.

I was falling in love.

Whenever you weren't sleeping, I played with you.
I put silly hats on you and took your picture.
I stared at you while you napped. (I know you were
really awake and just pretended to be asleep so you
could get some rest.)

On the long trip home you stood up in your seat and smiled at the man behind us. You charmed the flight attendants and slept like an angel as we flew through the clouds. It was the end of one amazing journey and the beginning of another.

When we finally landed, your new grandparents, aunts, uncles, cousins, and friends were waiting for you with lots of hugs and kisses.

Everyone wanted to look at you.

Your smallest cousin gently touched your little hand.

You cried when others took you from my arms and stopped when they brought you back.

You and I had become so close so quickly.

Your new room was filled with toys, stuffed animals, and a new crib. All the grownups watched as you carefully checked out your new room.

Then you smiled as if to say "I'm home."

Flowers, cards, and presents arrived. More and more people came to visit you.

But when they all left and that first day turned to night, I took you to your room, played a lullaby, and rocked you to sleep.

I held you tightly, kissed you softly, and cried.

The tears were for your Chinese mother, who could not keep you.

I wanted her to know that we would always remember her.

And I hoped somehow she knew you were safe and happy in the world.

The character for "love"
has the Chinese radical
meaning "heart" at its center.